Gearhead Garage

LOWRIDERS

DEANNA CASWELL

WORLD BOOK

BOLT

This World Book edition of *Lowriders*
is published by agreement between
Black Rabbit Books and World Book, Inc.
© 2018 Black Rabbit Books,
2140 Howard Dr. West,
North Mankato, MN 56003 U.S.A.
World Book, Inc.,
180 North LaSalle St., Suite 900,
Chicago, IL 60601 U.S.A.

Marysa Storm, editor; Grant Gould, interior designer; Michael Sellner,
cover designer; Omay Ayres, photo researcher

Library of Congress Control Number: 2016049941

ISBN: 978-0-7166-9306-2

Printed in the United States at CG Book Printers,
North Mankato, Minnesota, 56003. 3/17

CONTENTS

CHAPTER 1

Traveling in Style

People stop and watch as lowriders roll down the street. Pumps whine. Sound systems thump. The cars rise, lower, and bounce. Their **chrome** parts shine in the sun.

What Is a Lowrider?

Lowriders are cars that have been **modified**. But the changes don't make the cars faster. Instead, the changes let the cars ride low to the ground. The changes also add parts to lift the cars up and down.

Lowriders are usually older cars. The owners fix them up. They repair dents. They give the cars cool paint jobs. Each car is different.

By the Numbers

BSW 241

1,265

NUMBER OF CARS AT THE 2015 TORRES EMPIRE LOWRIDER SUPERSHOW

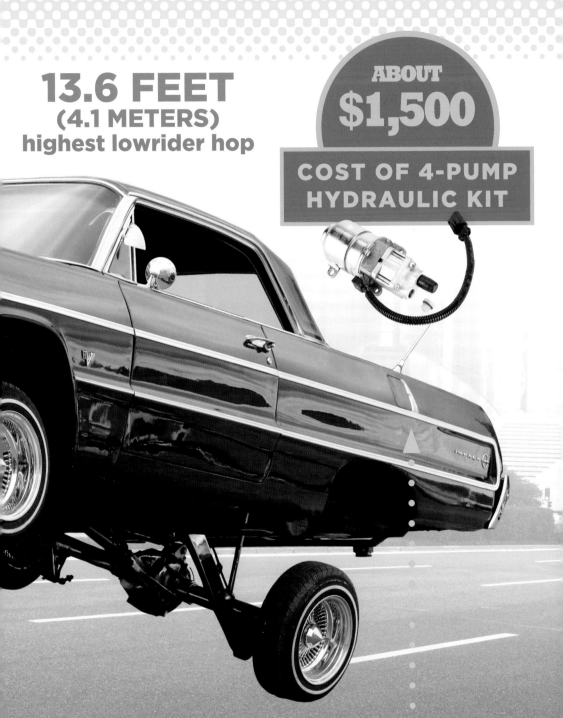

13.6 FEET
(4.1 METERS)
highest lowrider hop

ABOUT
$1,500

COST OF 4-PUMP HYDRAULIC KIT

ABOUT $10,000
COST OF LOWRIDER'S PAINT JOB

CHAPTER 2

The History of

After World War II, cars became very popular in the United States. Many people rushed to make **hot rods**. At the same time, Mexican Americans worked on cars that were low and slow. The cars were built for cruising. Owners wanted their cars to be personal and **unique**.

To lower cars, people put sandbags in them. The weight pressed the cars' bodies down.

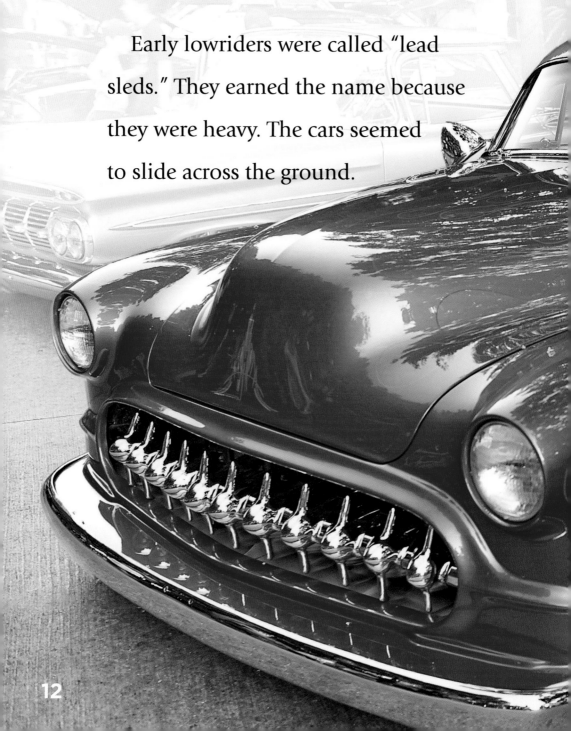

Lead Sleds

Early lowriders were called "lead sleds." They earned the name because they were heavy. The cars seemed to slide across the ground.

Many lead sleds were 1950 Mercurys.

Early lowriders used the same hydraulics as planes.

The First Lowrider

In the 1950s, people **discriminated** against Mexican Americans. And many people thought lowriders meant trouble. In 1958, California lawmakers made lowered cars illegal.

The law didn't stop driver Ron Aguirre. He put hydraulics in his car, X-Sonic. The system let him raise and lower the car. Then Aguirre could drive his car at the legal height.

X-Sonic was one of the first cars to use a lift system. Many people consider the car to be the first lowrider.

CHAPTER 3

Low and Slow

Today, all lowriders use air or hydraulic **suspensions**. Air suspensions use bags that fill with air to raise the car. The car lowers when the bag deflates.

Hydraulics let a car rise and lower quickly. Batteries in the car's trunk power the system. The system uses fluid to push the car up. The driver uses switches to control the height.

PARTS OF A LOWRIDER

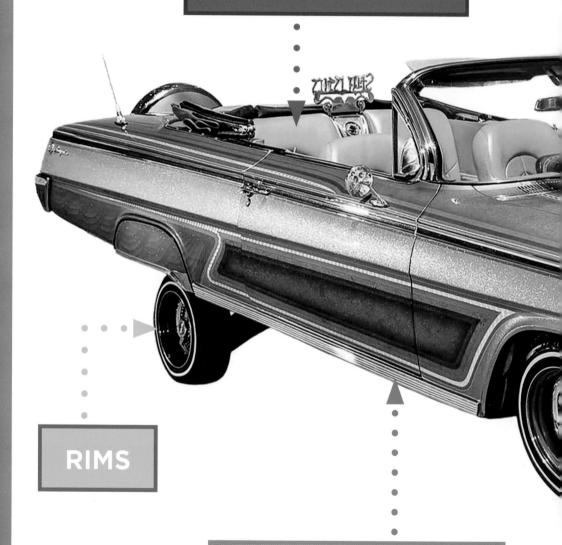

FANCY INTERIOR

RIMS

LOWERED FRAME

CUSTOM PAINT JOB

CHROME

NARROW TIRES

Hopping and Dancing

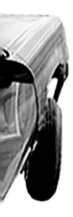

Today, lowriders don't just rise and lower. Drivers move them in many fun ways. Some compete in hop contests. People organize dance contests too. Owners perform a list of moves. These moves can include the hop front and hop back.

Cars in dance contests are judged. Judges watch for speed, height, rhythm, and switch control. Judges also look at the cars' overall performances.

Art on Wheels

Many lowriders impress people without even moving. Often, their paint jobs are enough to make people stop and stare.

Lowriders are works of art. Each paint job is different. Painters make multi-color designs. **Murals** make the cars stand out even more.

Types of Paint Jobs

Lowriders have many types of paint jobs.

metal flakes

pinstripes

fades

CHAPTER 4

The Future of Lowriders

Lowriders have changed a lot over the years. The technology used to raise the cars has gotten better. More people are interested in lowriders too. Today, lowriders are even on display in museums.

25

Cruising On

Many cities have lowrider clubs. Shows happen all across the United States. At shows, owners display their cars. The cars are becoming popular in other countries too. Lowriders will continue to impress people for years to come. They will always be

fancy and fun.

late 1950s

1949–1951

lead sled
model years

People begin
using lift
systems.

1940 |||||||||||||||||||||||||||||||||||||||

World War
II ends.

The first
people
walk on
the moon.

1945

1969

1977

Lowrider magazine comes out.

1992

Lowrider displays at the Smithsonian.

2000

Petersen Automotive Museum lowrider exhibit opens.

2005

The Mount St. Helens volcano erupts.

1980

2001

Terrorists attack the World Trade Center and Pentagon.

chrome (KROM)—a metal used to cover other metals to make them shiny

discriminate (dih-SKRIM-uh-neyt)—to unfairly treat a person or group of people differently from other people or groups

hot rod (HOT ROD)—a car that has been changed so that it can be driven and raced at very fast speeds

hydraulic (hahy-DRAW-lik)—a system that is operated through pressure or liquid

modify (MOD-uh-fahy)—to make changes

mural (MYOO-ruhl)—a usually large painting that is done directly on the surface of a wall or other object

suspension (suh-SPEN-shuhn)—the system of devices supporting the upper part of a vehicle on the axles

unique (yoo-NEEK)—very special or unusual

BOOKS

Aloian, Sam. *How a Car Is Made.* Engineering Our World. New York: Gareth Stevens Publishing, 2016.

Bailey, Diane. *How the Automobile Changed History.* Essential Library of Inventions. Minneapolis: Abdo Pub., 2015.

Dutta, Suneha. *Cars: Facts at Your Fingertips.* DK Pocket Genius. New York: DK Publishing, 2016.

WEBSITES

How to Draw a Lowrider
www.dragoart.com/tuts/2508/1/1/how-to-draw-a-lowrider-car.htm

Lowrider "Dave's Dream", 1992
americanhistory.si.edu/collections/search/object/nmah_1000887

Lowrider "Gypsy Rose" Featured in Chico and the Man Intro
www.kpbs.org/embedded/2012/may/16/3336/

INDEX